2019

For Madeleine,
Love, Aunt Joan

Dedication:

To my children, Josh (my heart), Kanani (my courage), Jacob (my soul), and Jenna (my light), May you change the world more than the world changes you.

To my hubby, Jeff who is also my Schmoopie, best friend, partner in all things, and favorite superhero, thank you for not only loving me for who I truly am, but for being the one who pushes me to live Pono.

Pono – Goodness, uprightness, true condition or nature
Nahoa – bold or defiant can also mean mental agony or extreme headache

ISLAND HERITAGE™
PUBLISHING
A DIVISION OF THE MADDEN CORPORATION

94-411 Kōʻaki Street
Waipahu, Hawaiʻi 96797-2806
Orders: (800) 468-2800
Information: (808) 564-8800
Fax: (808) 564-8877
welcometotheislands.com

ISBN: 1-61710-320-9
First Edition, Third Printing—2018
COP 180202

PONO
THE GARDEN GUARDIAN

Written by **Dani Hickman**
Illustrated by **Kristi Petosa-Sigel**

ISLAND HERITAGE™
PUBLISHING

Pono and his friends sneaked into Mrs. Miyamoto's yard long after the neighborhood had settled for the night. Pono and his people were tiny and went unseen by human giants when they made mischief. Mostly, they hid garden tools, moved lawn chairs, and did other silly things like dress up dogs in clothes left on the clothesline. Most of the little people enjoyed these pranks, but not Pono.

As they crept through the bushes, Pono asked his friend Nahoa, "Why do we do this every night?"

"Well," said Nahoa, "it's not as much fun as riding crabs, but it's still something to do."

"Riding crabs isn't fun either," said Pono. "They get really cranky when you hop on their backs and grab their eyes."

Following his friends into the garden, Pono picked up a rake and carried it to the far side of the yard. He had just finished uncoiling a garden hose across the grass when he heard something.

Mrs. Miyamoto's cat Neko had gotten out of the house and was heading right for them.

"Watch out!" Pono yelled as he began to run, "the cat!" Neko paused and turned toward Pono just long enough for Pono's friends to get away.

Now the cat focused on Pono. Pono ran toward a large bougainvillea bush and climbed into the middle, avoiding the sharp thorns. Neko tried to follow, but he couldn't get far without being poked.

Pono hoped Neko would give up, but instead, the cat sat back on its haunches and stared up at Pono through the branches. What was Pono going to do? He wiggled around and made himself as comfortable as he could for the long night to come.

7

Next morning Pono woke as a kindly voice called out, "Neko, time for breakfast. Where are you, kitty?"

Mrs. Miyamoto stepped into the backyard and frowned at the mess. Flower pots were flipped over, plants uprooted, and garden gnomes knocked down. Shaking her head, Mrs. Miyamoto reached for her rake, but it wasn't in its usual place; it was across the yard.

"That's strange. I always leave it right here," she thought, and she began walking over to get it.

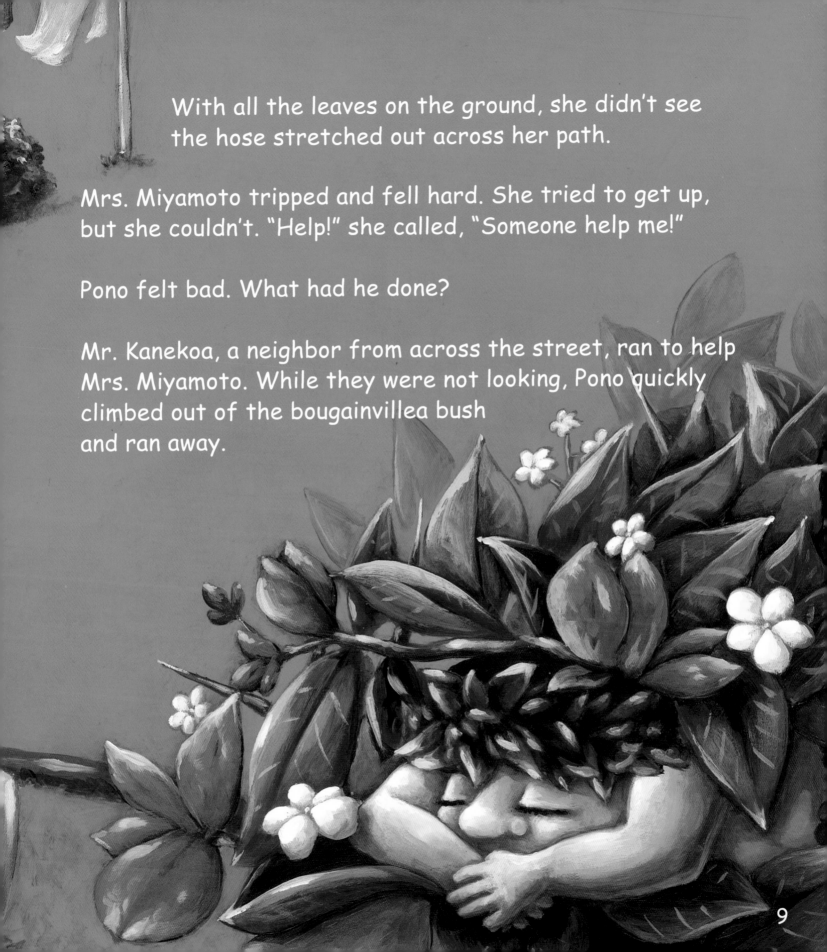

With all the leaves on the ground, she didn't see the hose stretched out across her path.

Mrs. Miyamoto tripped and fell hard. She tried to get up, but she couldn't. "Help!" she called, "Someone help me!"

Pono felt bad. What had he done?

Mr. Kanekoa, a neighbor from across the street, ran to help Mrs. Miyamoto. While they were not looking, Pono quickly climbed out of the bougainvillea bush and ran away.

When Pono got to his village, Kupuna, one of the elders, called him over.

"Pono, what's going on?" Kupuna asked

"Nothing, I just need some sleep." Pono shrugged and didn't look up.

Kupuna said, "Pono, all your life you've never spoken an untrue word to me. Is this the day you are going to start?"

Pono sighed and told the whole story. His voice was filled with guilt as he asked, "Why do we go out every night to make trouble? The others say it's fun, but I don't think it's fun at all."

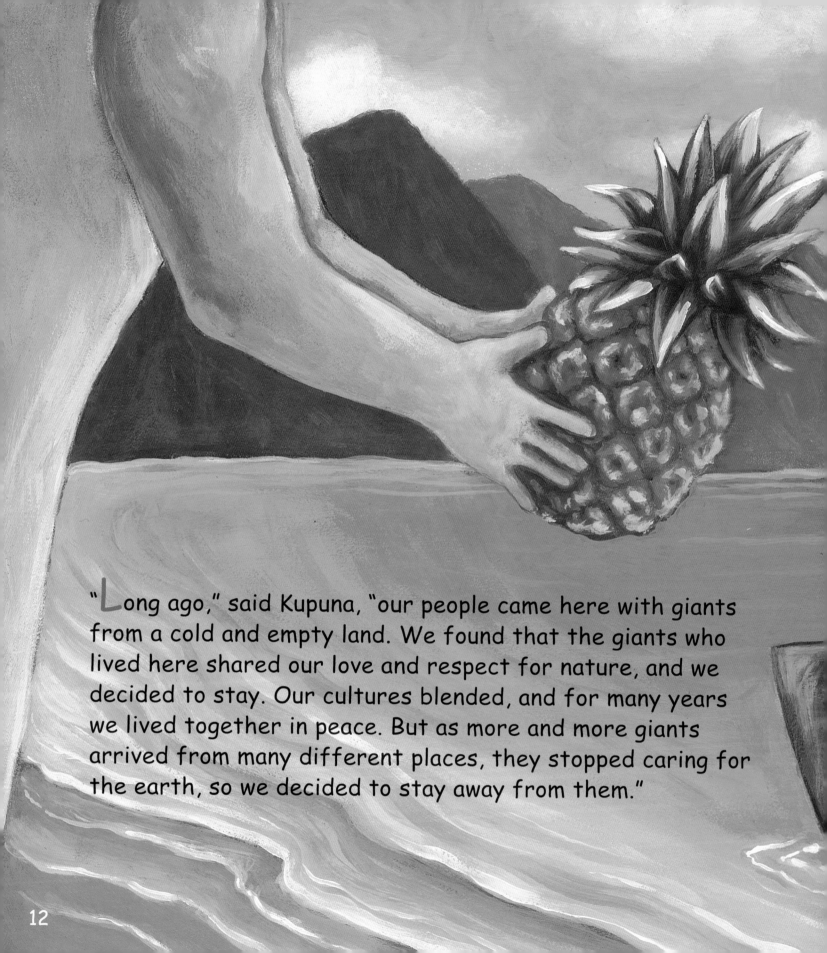

"Long ago," said Kupuna, "our people came here with giants from a cold and empty land. We found that the giants who lived here shared our love and respect for nature, and we decided to stay. Our cultures blended, and for many years we lived together in peace. But as more and more giants arrived from many different places, they stopped caring for the earth, so we decided to stay away from them."

"Our people were very disappointed and angry with the giants, and our young ones began to play tricks on them. No one tried to stop the mischief makers." said Kupuna. "Every new generation continued the troublemaking, and after a while, they forgot why they were doing it."

Kupuna continued, "Pono, who do you want to be? Your friends are doing things that do not speak to your heart. Remember, how you act is your choice."

That night Pono sat under the stars and came to a decision.
Tomorrow, he would become a new Pono....the right Pono.

When Pono approached the house next morning, Mrs. Miyamoto and her granddaughter Maya were talking to Mr. Kanekoa in the driveway.

"Thank you for your help yesterday, Mr. Kanekoa," Maya said. "The doctor says that grandma broke her foot and needs to rest."

Mrs. Miyamoto said, "I'm fine. I don't know what all the fuss is about."

"I'm glad you're okay Mrs. Miyamoto," said Mr.Kanekoa. "Don't worry. We'll all pitch in with the yard work."

Pono knew Mrs. Miyamoto was hurt because of what he had done. He needed to make things right. He sneaked past the giants as they continued talking.

Pono had gotten a good start on the cleanup by the time Maya came into the backyard.

She smiled and said, "Oh! It looks like grandma's neighbors are taking great care of the garden." Satisfied, Maya turned and walked back the way she came.

Pono watched her from behind the guava tree, "Perfect," he thought. "Everyone will think someone else is helping. The giants will not be suspicious. This is going to work."

Day after day, Pono tended to the garden as Neko the cat watched him from the window. Pono started bringing his ʻōʻō, a long pointed digging stick, to help break up the soil and pull stubborn weeds. He gathered seeds to replace damaged plants and fed the extras to the sparrows. In turn, the birds would help pick up fallen leaves and twigs. Pono made friends with the bees, who pollinated the flowers, and the geckos, who got rid of flies and gnats.

One day Pono heard a loud buzzing, but he wasn't concerned. He thought the bees had brought more friends to help out. But the buzzing wasn't the bees; it was something much more dangerous.

A huge hornet was circling above the garden. This was not good. Hornets by nature were grumpy. Mrs. Miyamoto would be in danger of being stung, and Pono could not let that happen.

He grabbed his 'ō'ō and shook it angrily at the hornet. The hornet charged at Pono, trying to get him with his big stinger. Pono swung his only weapon, determined to defend the garden.

Soon Pono was not alone. His friends the sparrows swooped and pecked at the intruder. The bees buzzed in, distracting the hornet with stingers of their own. Clearly outnumbered, the hornet flew away. Pono felt very grateful for his new friends.

The next day a heavy storm raged. The wind blew so hard that leaves and rain flew sideways through the village. Pono began to worry. His friends, the sparrows and bees and geckos....were they going to be okay? What was going to happen to the garden?

As soon as the weather cleared, Pono hurried to the garden. He gasped when he saw what had happened. Leaves and broken branches were everywhere. Mrs. Miyamoto's garden decorations were scattered all around, and pools of water flooded most of the yard. Pono felt so hopeless he turned around and went home.

Pono approached Kupuna, who was resting under a tree outside the village.

"All that work!" Pono cried. "The garden is destroyed! What was the point of all that? It doesn't make any sense.

Kupuna calmly replied, "Yes, it doesn't make sense." Pono brushed tears from his cheeks as Kupuna continued. "It doesn't make sense that you would walk all the way over there to plant flowers and pick up someone else's leaves. Was this about you being a gardener or you becoming a guardian? Pono, you could not have stopped the storm. The question is, is there nothing you can do now?"

Kupuna got up and walked away, leaving Pono deep in thought. By afternoon, his choice was clear. Pono raced back to the garden.

He was shocked to find his entire village hard at work, clearing, planting, and putting things back in their places. Because of everyone's efforts, the garden looked like it had before the storm.

Nahoa came and stood beside him. "Hey, Pono. I was thinking we should put in a cockroach race track near the plumeria tree over there." Pono smiled and shook his head. Nahoa went on, "Are you sure? Those buggahs run fast. It would be fun!"

Pono laughed. "I think Mrs. Miyamoto would notice if a lot of cockroaches were running around in her yard."

"Oh yeah, I guess you're right," said Nahoa. He turned with a shrug and continued cleaning up.

A muffled voice from inside the house was the villagers' only warning to hide as the back door began to open.

"Okay Neko, let's see how bad it is." Mrs. Miyamoto came out of the house and looked around in surprise.

"Neko, did you sneak out here when I wasn't looking and do some yardwork?" She giggled at her own silliness. "Maybe you had a little help."

She paused for a moment "...Or maybe a lot of help." Then, as if Mrs. Miyamoto could see the little people in the bushes, she said in a soft voice, "The garden has never looked more beautiful. Thank you."

The villagers heard Mrs. Miyamoto, and pride glowed on all their faces. Pono's heart was full. He had chosen the Pono he wanted to be.

He was Pono, the Garden Guardian.

The End